# Hide-and-Seek
# Birthday

Story by Ginny O'Donnell

Illustrations by Lynn Sweat

**Bantam Books**
**Toronto • New York • London • Sydney • Auckland**

**Today is Sam's birthday.**
**Who has he invited to his party?**

Bobby

Billy

Harry

Lisa

"Let's play Hide-and-Seek!" the children shout.
"Sam, you're It!"
Who is hiding already?

Sam

Lily

"Here I come, ready or not!"
What's that bump in the bed?
Is it Lily?

"I'll look in the attic!
It's full of secret places to hide.
Come out, come out!"

Sam looks in the hall closet.
He sees some hats and coats.
"I can see someone in the closet!"

In the backyard, Sam hears giggling.
"Who's in my tree house?"

"ACHOO!"
Sam turns around fast.
"Who is in Bonkers' house?"

**Back inside, Sam searches his room.
"Who's behind my blackboard?"**

"One, two, three, four...
who's behind the pantry door?
Isn't Lisa wearing a green dress?"

"Dad, have you seen Lisa? I've looked everywhere!"

"Here's Bonkers!
He's calling us to have some birthday cake!"
Now everyone has been found!

"Happy Birthday, Sam!" shout all the children.
"WOOF! WOOF!" says Bonkers.